This book is dedicated to kids everywhere
who have the fortitude to overcome daily challenges
and to reach their potential.

For Shannon and Quinn, who are not afraid to share
the importance of healthy eating with a generation that
desperately needs to hear it.

Thanks to Mom and Dad for your continued support and
your passion for the Mitch Spinach project.

Special thanks to Hill & Brand Kids and SoFAB Media for
bringing Mitch Spinach to a wider audience.

First Edition, Published by Mitch Spinach Productions, Inc.

Printed in the United States
ISBN 978-0-578-11158-2

Library of Congress Control Number:
2012948220

Mitch Spinach and The Tree House Intruder

by Hillary Feerick & Jeff Hillenbrand
in collaboration with Joel Fuhrman, M.D.
illustrated by Jorge Ortega

Mitch Spinach Productions, Inc.

Multicolored sprinkles covered the desk as Max popped doughnut after doughnut into his mouth, barely taking the time to chew. He had just finished a caramel candy bar when Ms. Radicchio asked her students to take out their pencils and get ready for math.

Max felt a little jittery. "Please sit still in your seat, Max," said Ms. Radicchio. "You're bouncing all over the place. Try to focus on the math lesson."

As Max apologized, he heard Billy snickering in the back row. Max felt as if the whole class was laughing at him.

As the day wore on, things only got worse for Max. In P.E., Mrs. Persimmon rewarded Isabella and Logan for being good listeners and let them pick the players for the dodge ball teams. Max hated this part of gym class. He was always picked last.

"Why is *your* hand raised, Max?" teased Billy. "The only game you could win is a pie-eating contest!"

Max felt like crying.

At the sound of Mrs. Persimmon's whistle, balls flew wildly across the gym. Billy aimed straight for Max and hit him right in the belly. He was the first one out *again*. Sitting on the sidelines, Max was tired of being Max.

Instead of crying, Max watched Mitch Spinach. He was incredible! Holding one ball, he spun around and jumped three feet into the air to catch another—Billy was out!

With amazing accuracy, Mitch Spinach fired the two balls at the same time, hitting Morgan and Riley—Both were out! "Wow! Those fruits and veggies really do give him super powers," thought Max.

4

For the rest of the day, Max imagined what it would be like to have super powers.

As Max lined up for the school bus, Billy was right behind him. "Hey Max, I don't think you're gonna fit through the door," sneered Billy.

"Leave me alone," pleaded Max as he climbed into the front seat behind Mr. Turmeric, the bus driver.

"That's enough, Billy," said Mr. Turmeric sternly. "You need to stop teasing Max. I'm going to have to speak to Principal Lycopene about your behavior."

Max sat by himself, as usual, still thinking about Mitch Spinach and the amazing things he could do. "What would happen," Max wondered, "if I knew his secrets about super foods? Would I become stronger, faster, and smarter like Mitch Spinach? Would Billy stop bothering me?"

Later that afternoon at Sunchoke Elementary, Mitch Spinach sat in Principal Lycopene's office discussing a school bully.

"There is an intruder in the tree house . . . there is an intruder in the tree house," repeated a robotic voice coming from Mitch Spinach's blue and green oversized watch. He pressed a large red button to silence the alarm.

"I'm sorry, Principal Lycopene," Mitch Spinach said. "My sister, Molly, is sending me an emergency message, and I need to get home right away."

"OK, but be careful,"
replied Principal Lycopene.

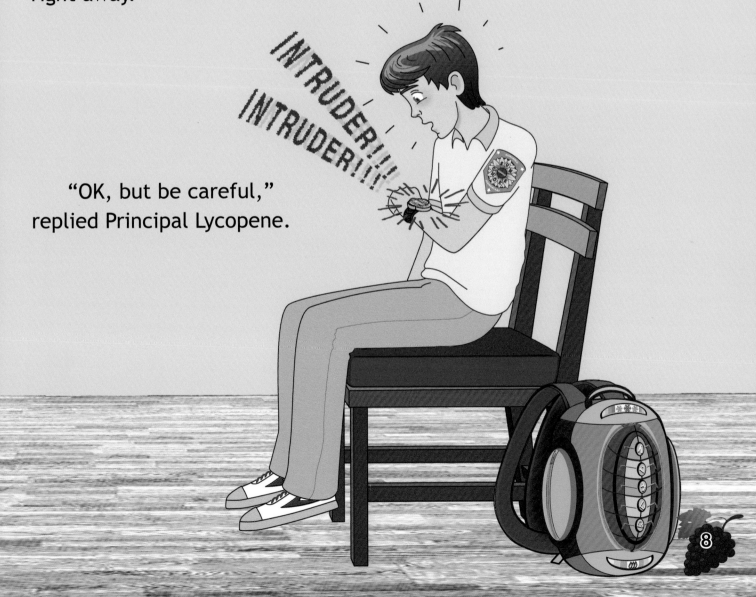

At 27 Cremini Way, Mitch and Molly Spinach searched the backyard for signs of the tree house intruder. Both of them had extraordinary eyesight from eating lots of cauliflower, sunflower seeds, and spinach. From one hundred feet away, they could see that the tree house was empty, but they walked quietly on their tiptoes, just in case. Something shiny sparkled on the ground; it was one of their homemade super bars, lying among the tangled roots of a one-hundred-year-old banyan tree.

In this old tree, Mitch and Molly had built an incredible treehouse in the shape of a giant red pepper. The roof was outfitted with glass panels that used the sun's energy to power the secret equipment inside. With a hidden periscope, satellite dish, and quick-escape banana slide, it was the most amazing tree house in the world!

Mitch Spinach climbed the rungs of the ladder to the carved wooden door. Molly Spinach grabbed a vine and climbed up in less than ten seconds without using her feet! Like her brother, she was incredibly strong!

Inside the tree house, it was quiet. An industrial-sized steel mixer and a powerful blender sat on a rectangular worktable. Recycled glass lights hanging from the ceiling shone on a convection oven whose black conveyor belt was loaded with freshly made super bars—but two of them had been stolen!

NIGHT-VISION

BRAINPOWER

NIGHT-VISION

SUPER-SONIC HEARING

BRAINPOWER

SUPER-SONIC HEARING

NUTS & SEEDS

Mitch and Molly scanned the walls of their tree house laboratory, which were covered with pictures of super foods and lists of superpowers—brainpower, concentration, muscle building, night vision, super-sonic hearing, and more.

"Look at this," said Molly Spinach. "Some of your new recipes are missing."

"Strange," replied Mitch Spinach. "I wonder who would have done this."

A moment later, Mitch Spinach noticed something else: a pencil with a French fry eraser was lying in the corner next to their barrel of protein-packed nuts and seeds.

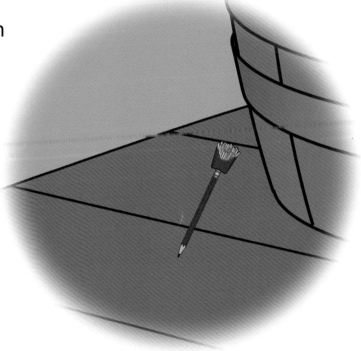

"Hmm, I feel like I've seen this pencil before, but I'm not sure where," murmured Mitch Spinach.

Mitch Spinach was still thinking about the tree house intruder when his class took its snack break the next day. He unzipped a side pocket in his Nutripak lunchbox, grabbed a shiny stainless steel container, and unscrewed the top.

"Mmm, your snack smells so good," said Kayla. "What are those?"

"Chickpea Power Bites, one of my favorite super foods! Chickpeas are loaded with protein that builds strong muscles and fiber that keeps you lean, but, most importantly, they're delicious. Here, try some."

"I'd love to," replied Kayla, popping a handful in her mouth. "These are awesome! I am going to ask my mom to buy some chickpeas."

14

"Hey Max, what are you eating over there?" asked Billy, butting into the conversation. "A box of candy bars?"

"No," said Max, turning in the other direction. "I'm not. Just leave me alone."

"OK everyone, settle down," instructed Ms. Radicchio. "Take out your math books and pencils, please."

Does anyone have a pencil I can borrow?" asked Mitch Spinach. "Mine just broke."

"I do," said Max, as he handed Mitch Spinach a pencil with a large hamburger eraser.

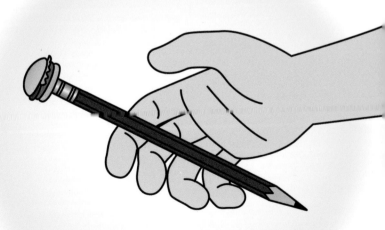

"Thanks for being such a good helper, Max," said Ms. Radicchio. "It's your turn to answer number six. What is 24 times 16?"

Max solved the problem in a flash. "Umm . . . 384, I think," he answered. Max's classmates were surprised.

"Correct!" said Ms. Radicchio. "You did that so fast! How about 12 times 26?"

"Uhh, umm, 312?" answered Max, hoping he was right.

"That's correct! Nice job, Max! You must have had a great snack today. You're so much more focused than usual. Keep up the good work," said Ms. Radicchio with a smile. Max smiled back and sat up a little straighter.

On the way out the door to recess, Mitch Spinach saw something in the trash that caught his eye. It was a wrapper from one of his homemade super bars. "Hmm, that's strange," thought Mitch Spinach. "I didn't have one of my super bars today."

Outside on the field, Mitch Spinach typed a message to Molly on his futuristic watch:

Meet me at the bike rack immediately after school. I have discovered 2 more clues that will help us solve the mystery of the tree house intruder.

*Meet me at the bike rack immediately after school. I have discovered 2 more clues that will help us solve the mystery of the tree house intru_*

1234567890
QWERTYUIOP
ASDFGHKLZX
@ !

Pedaling as fast as they could to keep up with the bus, Mitch and Molly Spinach arrived at the bus stop just as the kids were getting off.

Through the window, Max noticed Mitch and Molly on the sidewalk.

"Hi, Mitch. Hi, Molly. How are you guys doing?" stammered Max.

"Actually, we wanted to ask you something, Max," said Mitch Spinach.

"Uh, OK," he answered, starting to sweat.

"Yesterday, someone broke into our tree house, and all of the clues point to you," explained Mitch Spinach.

"What? What clues?" asked Max sharply.

"Well, the first clue we found was one of our homemade super bars lying on the grass under the tree house. Inside, we noticed that two super bars were missing from the conveyor belt and several of my new recipes had been stolen."

"So what? That doesn't mean I was the intruder," said Max defensively.

"You're right, but then we found a pencil that had rolled in the corner of the tree house. The tree house intruder must have been copying down some of my secret recipes and dropped it. I knew that I had seen that pencil somewhere before, but I couldn't remember where . . . until you loaned me your hamburger pencil today. It was *your* French fry pencil in our tree house, wasn't it, Max?"

"Lots of people have French fry pencils," said Max feebly.

"Yes, that's true," agreed Mitch Spinach, "and it wasn't until I noticed one of my super bar wrappers in the trash that I realized you were the intruder. I believe you ate a super bar at snack time today, and it super-charged your brain. You were amazing!

You answered all of Ms. Radicchio's questions easily because you hadn't eaten your usual candy and junk food. All that sugar affects your concentration."

Max looked at his shoes and took a deep breath. "You're right," said Max, looking away. "I am really, really sorry!" Tears rolled down his cheeks.

Max explained that he was tired of being teased by Billy, tired of always getting picked last in P.E., and tired of being laughed at because he had trouble concentrating in school. "I had a crazy plan," Max explained. "I thought that if I ate the same super foods you eat, then, maybe, I could have super powers, too, and Billy would stop teasing me."

"It's not a crazy plan," said Mitch Spinach, trying to comfort Max. "Just look at what happened in math today when you ate a healthy snack."

Max stopped crying. "That's true," said Max. "I was so much more focused. I felt great, actually."

"Right! So, here's our plan, explained Mitch Spinach. I will teach you all about super foods and share my secret recipes with you. You will promise to stop eating tons of junk food and candy and start eating fresh fruits and veggies. As you fuel your body better, you will become stronger, faster, smarter, and lighter. And Molly will help you get into better shape. She was the state champion in gymnastics this year," said Mitch Spinach, smiling proudly at his little sister. "She can certainly teach you a few tricks, right Molly?"

"Definitely!" said Molly with a grin. She loved a challenge.

"And I think Billy is going to stop teasing you," said Mitch Spinach. "Principal Lycopene knows what Billy's been up to. Everything is going to be OK."

"You guys are great friends," said Max. "Thank you!"

22

So, Mitch Spinach taught Max about the powerful nutrients found in fruits and vegetables.

SUPER-SONIC HEARING

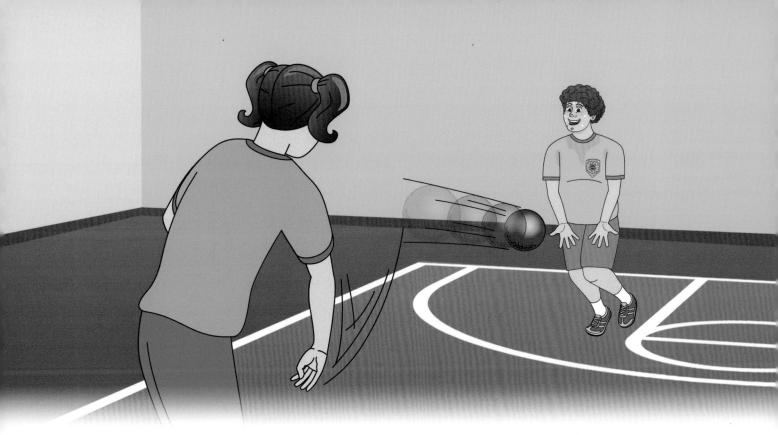

His sister, Molly, designed an exercise program that included rope climbing, hopping through hula-hoops, doing pushups and sit-ups, and catching red dodge balls.

24

Over the next three months, the kids in Room 201 noticed a change in Max. He replaced his usual chicken fingers and pepperoni pizza with healthy super foods. His junk food and candy bar snacks transformed into fruits, veggies, and Mitch Spinach super bars. Eating fruits and veggies made his brain work like a super computer.

Little by little, Max improved in P.E., too, especially in dodge ball. When Mrs. Persimmon blew her whistle, Max was ready to go.

One day, Billy fired his ball right at Max, but Max jumped two feet into the air and caught it. Billy couldn't believe his eyes. Max had gotten him out! Dodge balls flew back and forth, and Max caught half of them.

With amazing aim, Max hit Logan on the foot to win the game! Max couldn't believe how happy he felt to be Max as his teammates ran to give him big high-fives.

In the locker room, Billy gave Max a high-five, too. "Great game, Max," he exclaimed. "You were awesome!"

"Thanks," said Max, eyeing Billy cautiously.

Then, looking rather serious, Billy said quietly, "Hey Max, I feel really bad about having teased you for so long. I guess I didn't think about how it must have made you feel. I am really sorry."

"Apology accepted," replied Max, beaming.

After school at the bike racks, Mitch Spinach asked if Max wanted to help create a new super green smoothie recipe.

"Sounds great, but can we climb the rope first?" asked Max. "It's so much fun!"

"Absolutely!" said Mitch and Molly Spinach at *exactly* the same time.

SECRETS FOR PARENTS AND TEACHERS

After reading this book, children may ask "Can chickpeas make you super strong and lean?" or "Is junk food really bad for you?" These and other questions provide a great opportunity to explore the teaching message implicit in the Mitch Spinach mission:

Natural plant foods contain necessary and even essential components that enable optimal function of the human body, ensure maximum performance, and prevent against disease.

How do chickpeas make you strong and keep you lean?

Chickpeas, also called garbanzo beans and Egyptian peas, come in various sizes and colors and have a delicious nutty taste and creamy texture. Their Latin name, *cicer arietinum*, means "small ram" and reflects the unique shape of this legume that somewhat resembles a ram's head. Rich in protein, fiber, and micronutrients, chickpeas are a common ingredient in many Indian and Middle Eastern dishes and are available canned or dried. About 40% of the starchy carbohydrate in chickpeas is resistant to digestive enzymes and processed by bacteria in the digestive track into anti-inflammatory fatty acids. This conversion occurs so far down in the digestive track that about 90% of the calories in this "resistant starch" does not get absorbed, facilitating weight reduction. Chickpeas contain various types of phenolic acids and anthocyanins with powerful disease protective effects. They have a whopping 14 grams of protein per cup. When you get more protein from plant sources and less from animal sources you improve the anti-oxidant and fat profile of your diet in many ways and keep the hormone IgF-1 (insulinlike growth factor-one) in a favorable range. IgF-1 rises with protein sourced from animal products, and higher levels are thought to be a contributory cause of cancer.

Is junk food really bad for you?

Concentrated sweets enter the bloodstream rapidly with a surge of glucose that promotes the high secretion of insulin, the fat storage hormone. Insulin drives glucose uptake into our tissues, promoting the fabrication and storage of fat on the body. Since the processed carbohydrates (white flour and sugar) found in junk-food contain few micronutrients, they draw on the body's micronutrient storage as they are metabolized or burned for energy by the body. This process leads to nutritional deficiencies. In addition, these nutrient deficient foods lack anti-oxidant nutrients, phytochemicals, vitamins and minerals, so they create increased free radicals, inflammation and chronic damage to the body that eventually expresses itself as chronic disease. This damage may initially express itself not just with increased abdominal fat, but also with increased susceptibility to infection, fatigue, headaches, allergies, and attention difficulties. Eventually, the regular consumption of such refined foods results in chronic diseases and premature death.

Do you remember the name of the street on which Mitch and Molly live? They live at 27 Cremini Way. Cremini are powerful mushrooms that provide unique immune system support as they are rich in antioxidant and anti-inflammatory nutrients, including vitamins, B2, B3, B5, B6, B12, folate, and even some vitamin D. Mitch Spinach loves to eat crimini mushrooms, and you should, too!

Do you think Billy was a bully? Does he undergo any changes in the story? Why?
Bullying is unwanted, aggressive behavior among school age children. To learn more about bullying go to **www.StopBullying.gov**

Can eating fruits and veggies help you maintain a healthy weight and affect brain function?

The key to maintaining a healthy weight and performing your best is to eat predominantly foods that have a high proportion of micronutrients compared to calories. Most whole plant foods are rich in nutrients and low in calories, provide disease-preventive phytochemicals and satiating fiber, and promote overall health and a slim body without excess body fat. Studies have shown that people who eat more vegetables maintain their brain function as they age. Better memory and decision making abilities, and even happiness, are linked to a higher intake of plant produce. Like other organs of the body, the brain requires protective phytochemicals for healthy function.

How does carrying excess weight affect children's overall health?

When you fill up on low nutrient, calorie dense food, the resulting undernourishment leads to unrelenting appetite and food cravings, inducing more overeating. Low nutrient foods have addictive properties; they activate dopamine reward circuits (addictive drives and cravings) in the brain and produce withdrawal symptoms, which are often mistaken for hunger (headaches, fatigue, weakness, etc.), and therefore promote overconsumption of calories. High nutrient eating, consuming fruits, vegetables, beans, seeds and nuts, with their full symphony of natural micronutrients, helps to resolve food addictions, cravings, and withdrawal symptoms, so people are not driven to consume more calories than their bodies need. Burgers, fries, soda and other similar fast food choices are very high in calories but contain almost no micronutrients (vitamins, minerals and phytochemicals). Eating this type of food makes us want to eat more and more, making us sicker and sicker. Much like cigarettes or illegal drugs, high calorie, junk food is addictive. We feel ill if we don't have another soda or more fries to get our fix of oil, sugar, salt, and caffeine. We are over-eating, but our bodies are starving for micronutrients. The resulting excess fat on the body causes further inflammation and blocks insulin action. It forces the pancreas to overwork and produce too much insulin, leading to more weight gain and eventually diabetes, heart disease and more accelerated damage to the body as the years progress.

SOME SECRETS ABOUT A FEW OF THE CHARACTERS IN THIS BOOK

Mr. Turmeric is named after a plant that grows wild in the forests of Asia. A richly-colored, yellow powder is made from its roots, and it has been used in Indian and Asian cuisine for thousands of years. Today, active research is being pursued for many therapeutic purposes of turmeric, and its active ingredient, curcumin, has been shown to have anti-inflammatory and immune system benefits that protect against cancer and later-life dementia.

Ms. Radicchio is named after a burgundy leafed vegetable said to be native to Italy. It is often used in salads and has a crunchy, nutty, pleasantly bitter taste that mellows when cooked. Radicchio is a rich source of dietary fiber, antioxidants, vitamins, and minerals.

Mrs. Persimmon's name comes from a delicious red-orange fruit originally grown chiefly in Asia, rich in vitamins, minerals, and the proanthocyanidin class of antioxidants, which has anti-cancer and longevity benefits. The skin of the persimmon is also edible, nutritious, and delicious, so eat the entire fruit, except the green stem.

Principal Lycopene is named after a very efficient antioxidant responsible for the red pigment found in tomatoes, guava, pink grapefruit and watermelon. Lycopene can neutralize oxygen-derived free radicals that can cause damage to the body and are linked to many degenerative diseases, such as cardiovascular diseases, premature aging, cancer (especially prostate cancer), and cataracts.

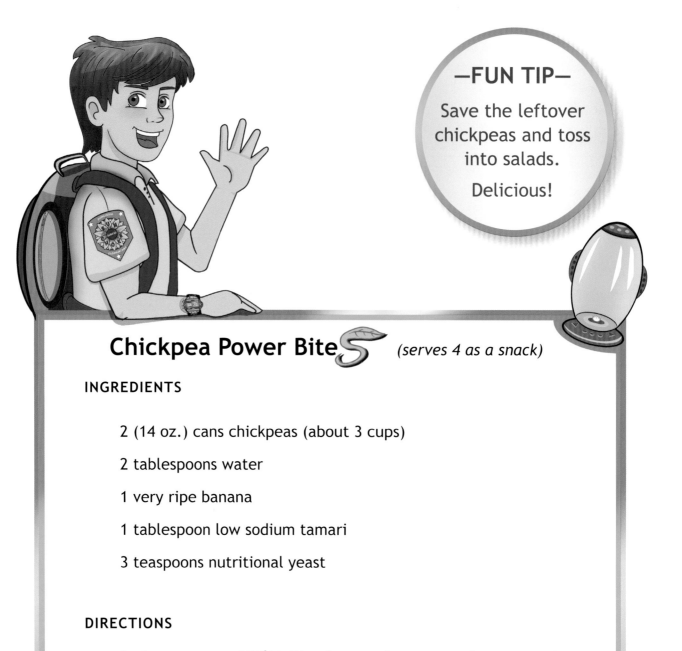

—FUN TIP—

Save the leftover chickpeas and toss into salads.

Delicious!

Chickpea Power Bite*S* *(serves 4 as a snack)*

INGREDIENTS

2 (14 oz.) cans chickpeas (about 3 cups)

2 tablespoons water

1 very ripe banana

1 tablespoon low sodium tamari

3 teaspoons nutritional yeast

DIRECTIONS

Preheat oven to 350˚F. Blend water, banana, and tamari with an immersion blender or a traditional one. Coat chickpeas with mixture and sprinkle with nutritional yeast. Toss and spread onto rimmed baking sheet lined with parchment paper. Bake for 20-30 minutes, tossing occasionally. For a more savory version (sometimes preferred by parents), eliminate the banana and simply toss the chickpeas with 2 tablespoons low sodium tamari and 1 teaspoon nutritional yeast. Bake for 10-15 minutes at 350˚F. Enjoy!

For more great recipes, nutrition information, games, and Mitch Spinach secrets go to

www.MitchSpinach.com